Where are you SCRUFFY PUP?

This book belongs to

....

THIS STORY HAS...

Alfie

Amelia
She lives with her
mum, dad and
twin, Alfie

**Amelia's
mummy**

Jenny
The nursery worker

Grandad and Granny

Sock
Grandad and Granny's cat

Charlie
Amelia's friend

Read more books in this series:

Can I Slurp My Spaghetti?

My Turn, Your Turn

Swim Like A Fish

WHERE ARE YOU SCRUFFY PUP?

A LAUGHING LOBSTER BOOK 978-1-913906-99-3

Published in Great Britain by Laughing Lobster, an imprint of Centum Publishing Ltd.
This edition published 2023.

5 7 9 10 8 6

© 2021 Laughing Lobster, an imprint of Centum Publishing Ltd. All Rights Reserved.

Illustrations by Julia Seal.

Laughing Lobster, an imprint of Centum Publishing Ltd, 20 Devon Square, Newton Abbot, Devon, TQ12 2HR, UK. Centum Publishing Ltd, 9/10 Fenian St, Dublin 2, D02 RX24, Ireland

books@centumpublishingltd.co.uk

LAUGHING LOBSTER, CENTUM PUBLISHING LIMITED Reg. No. 08497203

A CIP catalogue record for this book is available from the British Library.

Printed in Great Britain.

Where are you SCRUFFY PUP?

Let's play hide and seek! Can you find
this umbrella hiding in the story 8 times?

It was a splishy, sploshy, rainy day. Amelia and her twin brother Alfie were going out on a nature walk with their nursery class.

Amelia pulled her wellies out of
the box next to the front door.
"Red for Alfie," she grinned. "And yellow ones for me!"
Mum helped the twins tuck in their trousers and button
up their coats.
"Let's go!" giggled Alfie. "I want to jump in puddles!"

Amelia and Alfie went to Little Caterpillars Nursery. They were going on the nature walk with all of their friends.

"Time to get in the car," said Mum, "can't be late today!"

"Wait!" cried Amelia. "I've forgotten something!"
She kicked off her wellies and rushed upstairs.

Amelia burst into her bedroom and scooped up a cuddly toy puppy.
"How could I forget you, Scruffy Pup?" she smiled.

Scruffy Pup was Amelia's best friend. Even though he had a patch on one eye and shabby fur, she loved him more than anything.

When Amelia got back down the stairs, Mum frowned.
"You can't take Scruff today," she said. "He'll get wet."
"But Mum!" said Amelia.
"Not today," replied Mum. "You might lose him."

Amelia felt sorry for Scruffy Pup. He didn't want to miss the nature walk.

"Shh!" she whispered.

Before anyone could see, she tucked him into her backpack and did up the zip.

"Hello Alfie! Hi Amelia!" Jenny, the Little Caterpillars helper, was waiting outside nursery. All of the children were lined up in pairs behind her, ready for the nature walk.

Alfie and Amelia gave Mum a kiss goodbye.
"Granny and Grandad are picking you up
today," she smiled. "Have fun!"

When everybody's name had been ticked off Jenny's list, it was time to go.

Amelia and Alfie saw ladybirds,

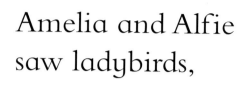

collected sticks,

looked under rocks

and jumped in lots of muddy puddles!

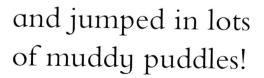

At the end of the nature walk, Granny and
Grandad arrived.

"Look at you both!" cried Granny.

"Two muddy children!" chuckled Grandad.

The twins couldn't wait to get to Granny and Grandad's.
"Can we visit the tomatoes?" asked Alfie, tugging
on Grandad's arm. Alfie and Grandad were growing
them in the greenhouse.
"OK," nodded Grandad. "Perhaps we can pick
one for tea."

"I'm going to say hello to Socks," decided Amelia.
Socks was Granny and Grandad's cat. He was
a bit shy sometimes. Luckily Amelia knew all
of his favourite hiding places.

"Found you!" said Amelia, peeping under Granny's bed. Socks stretched a furry paw out towards her. "Come out and say hello to Scruff," said Amelia.

Amelia unzipped her backpack, but Scruff was not there. "What?" she gasped.
She tipped everything out. Scruffy Pup had gone.

Amelia burst into the kitchen.

"Oh Granny!" she cried. "I've lost Scruff!"

Granny took off her washing-up gloves, then gave Amelia a cuddle.

"You must have left him at nursery," she decided.

Granny drove Amelia all the way back to
Little Caterpillars.
"Sorry," said Jenny. "Nothing's been handed in."
Scruffy Pup had disappeared.

When they got home again, Amelia climbed onto Granny's lap. She remembered the nature walk.

Perhaps poor Scruff was lying in a puddle right now, feeling cold and wet?

Alfie and Grandad came in from the garden.
"What's up?" asked Grandad.
"I've lost Scruffy Pup," sobbed Amelia, "Mummy told
me not to take him, but I did and now he's gone!"

When she got to nursery the next day, Amelia still felt sad. Charlie waved at her.

"Look," gasped Alfie. "He's got Scruff!"

"I found him," said Charlie proudly, "and I kept him safe all night."

Amelia gave Charlie a big hug. "Thank you!"

It was so good to have Scruffy Pup back again.

"I will look after you properly from now on," she whispered in his ear. "I promise!"

THE END

✳ CAN YOU REMEMBER?

What do Amelia and Alfie wear on their feet to go on the nursery nature walk?

Who does Amelia hide in her backpack?

What is Amelia and Alfie's nursery called?

Who picks them up from nursery?

Where is Socks the cat hiding?

Who finds and keeps Scruffy Pup safe for Amelia?

SAY GOODBYE TO...

Alfie

Amelia
She lives with her
mum, dad and
twin, Alfie

**Amelia's
mummy**

Jenny
The nursery worker

Grandad and Granny

Sock
Grandad and Granny's cat

Charlie
Amelia's friend

HOPE YOU ENJOYED
THE STORY!